THE BOXCAR CHILDREN®

MYSTERY BEHIND THE WALL

Time to Read® is an early reader program designed to guide children to literacy success regardless of age or grade level. The program's three levels correspond to stages of reading readiness, making book selection straightforward, and assuring that when it's time for a child to read, the right book is waiting.

— Level — 1

Beginning to Read

- Large, simple type
- Basic vocabulary
- Word repetition
- Strong illustration support

— Level — 2

Reading with Help

- Short sentences
- Engaging stories
- Simple dialogue
- Illustration support

— Level — 3

Reading Independently

- Longer sentences
- Harder words
- Short paragraphs
- Increased story complexity

Library of Congress Cataloging-in-Publication data is on file with the publisher.

Copyright © 2022 by Albert Whitman & Company
First published in the United States of America
in 2022 by Albert Whitman & Company
ISBN 978-0-8075-5455-5 (hardcover)
ISBN 978-0-8075-5458-6 (ebook)

THE BOXCAR CHILDREN® is a registered trademark
of Albert Whitman & Company.

TIME TO READ® is a registered trademark
of Albert Whitman & Company.

Printed in China
10 9 8 7 6 5 4 3 2 1 HH 26 25 24 23 22 21

Cover and interior art by Liz Brizzi

Visit The Boxcar Children® online at www.boxcarchildren.com.
For more information about Albert Whitman & Company,
visit our website at www.albertwhitman.com.

THE BOXCAR CHILDREN ®

MYSTERY BEHIND THE WALL

Based on the book by
Gertrude Chandler Warner

Albert Whitman & Company
Chicago, Illinois

It was a warm July day.

It had been a busy summer.

But Benny Alden was restless.

His friend Mike was on vacation.

His friend Rory lived too far away to play.

"I wish I could see my school friends," Benny told his dog, Watch.

Grandfather thought
something might be wrong.
Then at supper Benny barely
ate his food, and Grandfather
knew something was wrong.

Grandfather rubbed his
mustache in thought.
That night he made a plan.

The Alden children had not
always lived with Grandfather.
For a little while, they had lived
in a boxcar.
The Aldens had all kinds of
adventures in the boxcar.

Then Grandfather found them.
Now they had a real home,
and they still had all kinds of
adventures.

At breakfast the next day,
the children thought
Grandfather might have a
surprise for them.
He made some phone calls.
By lunchtime they *knew* he had
a surprise.
"Are we going on a trip?"
asked Violet.
"Are we going into town?"
asked Henry.
"We are not going anywhere,"
Grandfather said with a smile.
"Benny's friend Rory is coming
to visit!"

The children ran upstairs.
They loved having visitors.
Their big house had lots of
rooms.
Benny knew just which one
Rory should stay in:
the one down the hall with
the grandfather clock.
It was right next to his own.

As the children got the room
ready, Violet saw something
strange.

"This looks like a photo of our
house," she said.

"Who is this little girl?"

Grandfather explained.
Before he bought the house,
the Shaw family had lived there.
They had a girl named
Katharine.
"She looks sad," said Jessie.
"There weren't many kids her
age around," said Grandfather.
"Her mother tried to get her
to sew, to stay busy.
But Katharine liked collecting
things.
When they moved away,
they said she hid a coin
collection in the house.

But I have never seen it!"
The children looked at
one another.
Was there a mystery in their
very own house?

The next day, Rory arrived. Benny and Rory had a lot to talk about, and Rory loved to talk.

Benny barely ate his dinner. This time he was too busy talking to his friend.

They had so much to catch up on that they didn't want to stop talking.

At night they knocked on the walls of their closets, sending messages to each other in code.

In the morning, Benny and
Rory made a plan.
They would put a string
between their rooms.
They would tie a can to
each end.

When they spoke into the cans,
the string would carry their
voices.
They could talk all night!
The pair went upstairs,
past the grandfather clock,
and into Rory's room.

They looked for a space to put
the string.
Benny found a loose board
in the closet.
Pop! The board came off.
They could not find a place
to put a string.
But they did find a surprise…

Behind the wall was a cloth and a note.

The cloth had little slots sewed in it.

The stitching wasn't very good.

The note was from Katharine.
She *had* hidden her coins
in the house.
It was a treasure hunt!

Henry, Jessie, and Violet gathered around.

The first clue was very strange.

"Go to 5 Birds," it read.

"Five birds?" asked Benny.

"Where will we find five birds together after all this time?"

Henry had an idea.

"I don't think the note is about birds at all," he said.

The children followed Henry
on their bikes.
They came to a place called
5 Birds Lane.
The clue was an address!
It was a little sewing shop.
Inside was a woman named
Mrs. Wren.
They showed her the note,
but she just shook her head.
Then they showed her the cloth.
A big smile appeared on her face.
"This is where Katharine kept
her coins," she said.

"I would know that stitching anywhere," she chuckled.
The woman went to the back of the shop.
"I have something for you!"

Mrs. Wren showed them a note.

Katharine had given it to her long ago.

She was waiting for just the right people to give it to.

It was another clue!

"Attic, dollhouse," the clue read.

Benny scratched his head.

"Dollhouses are small.

Their attics are even smaller.

Not many coins would fit there."

"Not the dollhouse's attic,"
said Jessie.
"Our attic!"

The children hurried home.
They rushed up to the attic.
Sure enough, they found
an old dollhouse.
And sure enough, another clue
fell out.
This note read, "Grandfather's
door."

The children looked at one
another.
There were lots of doors
in the house.
And their grandfather was not
Katharine's grandfather.
Where could a note be hiding
after all this time?
They had no idea.

Grandfather's
door

That night Benny could not
sleep.

Next door, Rory could not sleep
either.

They both listened to the clock
in the hall and thought about
their mystery.

When the clock chimed,
they both had an idea.
The two met in the hallway.
"The clue is 'Grandfather's
door,'" said Benny.
"The door of the grandfather
clock!" said Rory.
There was another note inside!

In the morning, Benny and
Rory shared the note.
"'Last clue,'" Benny read.
"'Look on the back of the house.
But don't break the glass.'"
They were getting close!

The children went to the back
of their house.
"No clue could last out here,"
said Henry.
They went to the dollhouse
in the attic.
"There's no more clues here,"
said Violet.

The Aldens were close,
but they were stuck.
Two days passed.
Soon it would be time for Rory
to go home.
Would they be able to solve the
mystery in time?

Benny went to Rory's room.
The two sat on the old bed.
Benny was glad Rory had come
to visit, even if they didn't solve
the mystery.
Benny looked at the picture of
Katharine behind the glass.

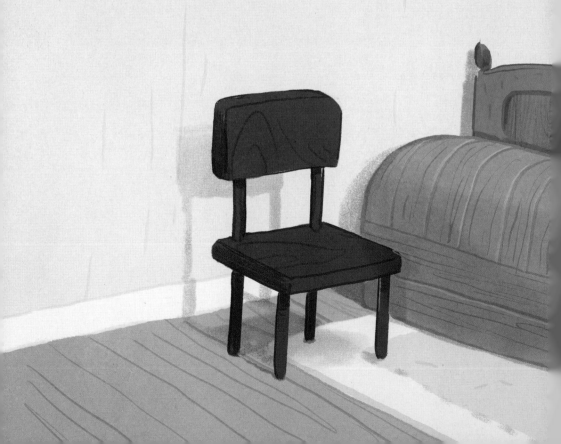

"She must have been lonesome in this big house," he said.
Rory stood up.
"I think I know the answer!"

Rory pointed to the picture of
the old house.

"I get it," said Benny. "The clue
said, 'on the back of the house'!"
Rory turned the picture over
so the glass was facing down.
"'Don't break the glass,'"
Rory said.
Could this be where the coin
collection was?

Together they opened the back
of the picture…

There were nickels and dimes,
quarters and pennies.
They had found it!
Together they showed the
others what they had found.

Then Benny made a pile for
Rory and a pile for himself.
"Are you sure you don't want
to keep it?" said Rory.
Benny shook his head.
He was happy to find
Katharine's collection…

but he was happier he could share it with a friend.

Keep reading with The Boxcar Children®!

Henry, Jessie, Violet, and Benny used to live in a boxcar. Now they have adventures everywhere they go! Adapted from the beloved chapter book series, these early readers allow kids to begin reading with the stories that started it all.

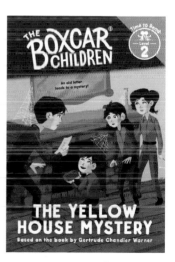

HC 978-0-8075-0839-8 · US $12.99
PB 978-0-8075-0835-0 · US $4.99

HC 978-0-8075-7675-5 · US $12.99
PB 978-0-8075-7679-3 · US $4.99

HC 978-0-8075-9367-7 · US $12.99
PB 978-0-8075-9370-7 · US $4.99

HC 978-0-8075-5402-9 · US $12.99
PB 978-0-8075-5435-7 · US $4.99

HC 978-0-8075-5142-4 · US $12.99
PB 978-0-8075-5139-4 · US $4.99

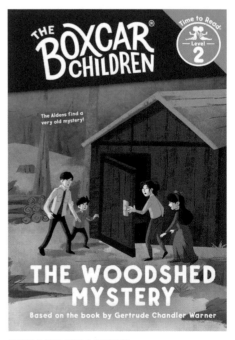

HC 978-0-8075-0795-7 · US $12.99
PB 978-0-8075-0800-8 · US $4.99

HC 978-0-8075-9210-6 · US $12.99
PB 978-0-8075-9216-8 · US $4.99

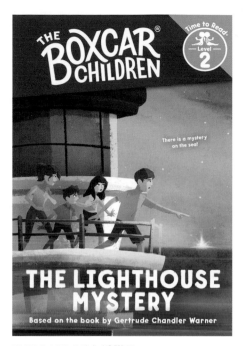

THE LIGHTHOUSE MYSTERY

Based on the book by Gertrude Chandler Warner

HC 978-0-8075-4548-5 · US $12.99
PB 978-0-8075-4552-2 · US $4.99

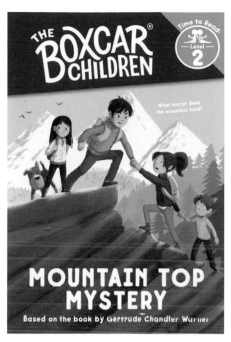

MOUNTAIN TOP MYSTERY

Based on the book by Gertrude Chandler Warner

HC 978-0-8075-5291-9 · US $12.99
PB 978-0-8075-5289-6 · US $4.99

SCHOOLHOUSE MYSTERY

Based on the book by Gertrude Chandler Warner

HC 978-0-8075-7261-0 · US $12.99
PB 978-0-8075-7259-7 · US $4.99

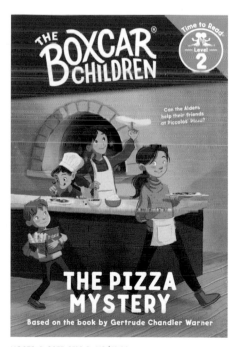

THE PIZZA MYSTERY

Based on the book by Gertrude Chandler Warner

HC 978-0-8075-6516-2 · US $12.99
PB 978-0-8075-6511-7 · US $4.99

GERTRUDE CHANDLER WARNER discovered when she was teaching that many readers who like an exciting story could find no books that were both easy and fun to read. She decided to try to meet this need, and her first book, *The Boxcar Children*, quickly proved she had succeeded.

Miss Warner drew on her own experiences to write the mystery. As a child she spent hours watching trains go by on the tracks opposite her family home. She often dreamed about what it would be like to set up housekeeping in a caboose or freight car—the situation the Alden children find themselves in.

While the mystery element is central to each of Miss Warner's books, she never thought of them as strictly juvenile mysteries. She liked to stress the Aldens' independence and resourcefulness and their solid New England devotion to using up and making do. The Aldens go about most of their adventures with as little adult supervision as possible—something else that delights young readers.

Miss Warner lived in Putnam, Connecticut, until her death in 1979. During her lifetime, she received hundreds of letters from girls and boys telling her how much they liked her books.